Dear Parents:

Congratulations! Your child is taking the first steps on an exciting journey. The destination? Independent reading!

STEP INTO READING® will help your child get there. The program offers five steps to reading success. Each step includes fun stories and colorful art or photographs. In addition to original fiction and books with favorite characters, there are Step into Reading Non-Fiction Readers, Phonics Readers and Boxed Sets, Sticker Readers, and Comic Readers—a complete literacy program with something to interest every child.

Learning to Read, Step by Step!

Ready to Read   Preschool–Kindergarten
• big type and easy words • rhyme and rhythm • picture clues
For children who know the alphabet and are eager to begin reading.

Reading with Help   Preschool–Grade 1
• basic vocabulary • short sentences • simple stories
For children who recognize familiar words and sound out new words with help.

Reading on Your Own   Grades 1–3
• engaging characters • easy-to-follow plots • popular topics
For children who are ready to read on their own.

Reading Paragraphs   Grades 2–3
• challenging vocabulary • short paragraphs • exciting stories
For newly independent readers who read simple sentences with confidence.

Ready for Chapters   Grades 2–4
• chapters • longer paragraphs • full-color art
For children who want to take the plunge into chapter books but still like colorful pictures.

STEP INTO READING® is designed to give every child a successful reading experience. The grade levels are only guides; children will progress through the steps at their own speed, developing confidence in their reading.

Remember, a lifetime love of reading starts with a single step!

For Tammy, my MOH
—M.L.

Step into Reading, Random House, and the Random House colophon are registered trademarks of Penguin Random House LLC.

Visit us on the Web!
StepIntoReading.com
randomhousekids.com

Educators and librarians, for a variety of teaching tools, visit us at RHTeachersLibrarians.com

ISBN 978-0-7364-3668-7 (trade) — ISBN 978-0-7364-8193-9 (lib. bdg.)
ISBN 978-0-7364-3669-4 (ebook)

Printed in the United States of America   10 9 8 7 6 5 4 3 2 1

STEP INTO READING®

2

STEP

READING WITH HELP

DISNEY
PRINCESS
A Dream for a Princess

by Melissa Lagonegro
illustrated by Pulsar Estudio

Random House 🏠 New York

There once was a girl
named Cinderella.
She was kind
and gentle.

Cinderella lived with
her wicked stepmother
and stepsisters.

She had many chores.

She served them tea.

She cooked their food.

She made their beds.

One day,
a letter came
from the palace.
"Come meet the Prince
at a royal ball," it said.

The stepsisters
were very excited.
Cinderella was, too!

Cinderella's stepmother
gave her more chores.
Cinderella did not
have time to make
a ball gown.

"Surprise!"
cried her little friends.
They had made her
a fancy gown.

"Now I can go
to the ball!"
cheered Cinderella.

Oh, no!
The stepsisters
tore her gown.
It was ruined!

Cinderella cried.

Piff, puff, poof!

Her fairy godmother

appeared.

"You cannot go
to the ball
like that," she said.

She waved
her magic wand.
<u>Poof!</u>

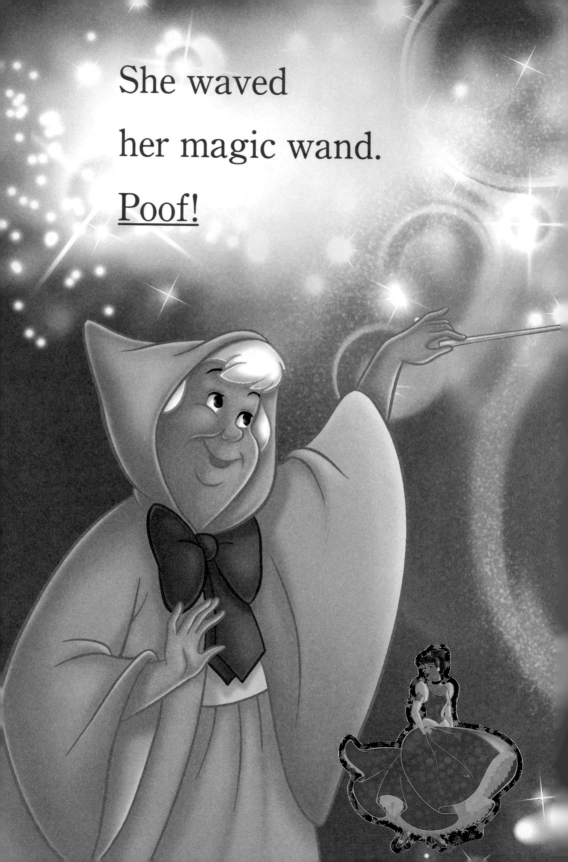

A royal coach.

White horses.

Two coachmen.

And a beautiful gown!

Cinderella was headed
to the ball!

Cinderella and the
Prince danced . . .

. . . and danced . . .

. . . and danced.

Her dream had come true.